AVALANCHE ANNIE

A NOT-SO-TALL TALE

Lisa Wheeler   ILLUSTRATED BY Kurt Cyrus

HARCOURT, INC.

Orlando   Austin   New York   San Diego   Toronto   London

For my lovely aunt, Christine Tkacs, who taught me
the importance of books, brains, and big dreams
—L. W.

Text copyright © 2003 by Lisa Wheeler
Illustrations copyright © 2003 by Kurt Cyrus

www.HarcourtBooks.com

Library of Congress Cataloging-in-Publication Data
Wheeler, Lisa, 1963–
Avalanche Annie: a not-so-tall tale by Lisa Wheeler; illustrated by Kurt Cyrus.
p. cm.
Summary: When the Yoohoos of northern Michisota are caught in an avalanche on
Mount Himalachia, little Annie Halfpint saves the day and earns a new nickname.
[1. Avalanches—Fiction. 2. Cowgirls—Fiction. 3. Size—Fiction. 4. Humorous stories.
5. Tall tales. 6. Stories in rhyme.] I. Cyrus, Kurt, ill. II. Title.
PZ8.3.W5665Av 2003
[E]—dc21 2001007825
ISBN 0-15-216735-8

First edition
H G F E D C B A

Printed in Singapore

The display lettering was created by Tom Seibert.
The text type was set in Galliard.
Color separations by Bright Arts Ltd., Hong Kong
Printed and bound by Tien Wah Press, Singapore
This book was printed on totally chlorine-free Enso Stora Matte paper.
Production supervision by Sandra Grebenar and Ginger Boyer
Designed by Kurt Cyrus and Judythe Sieck

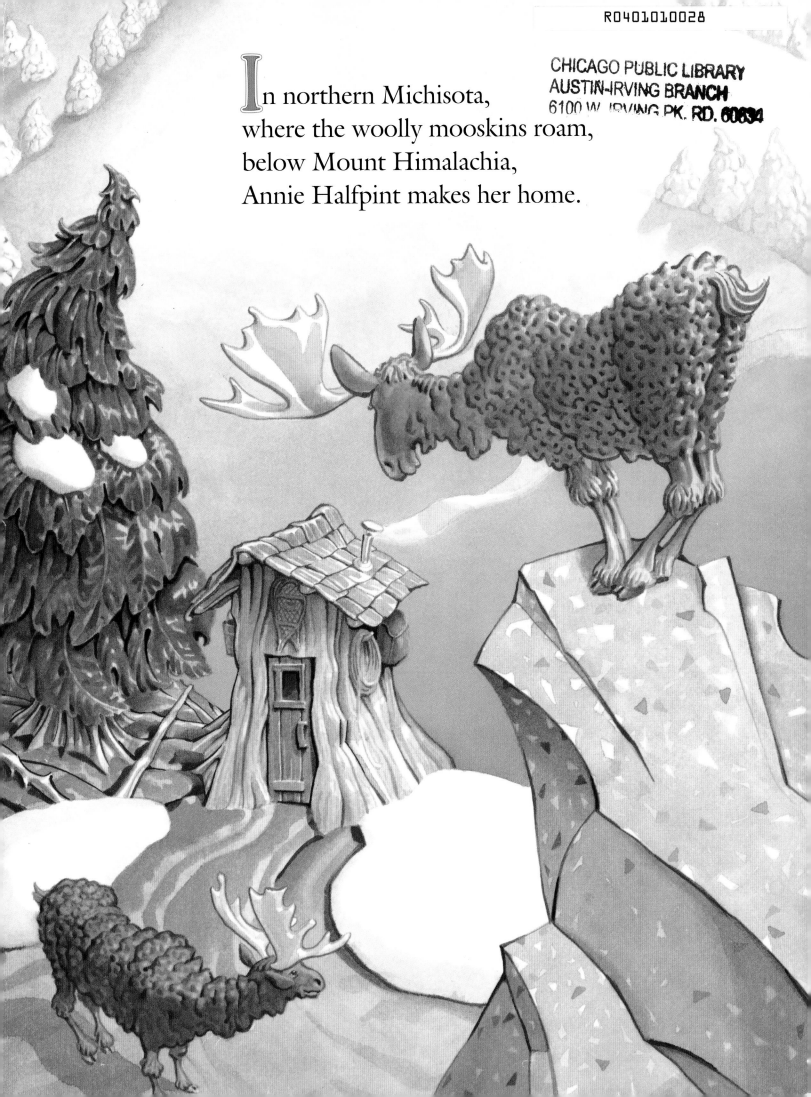

In northern Michisota,
where the woolly mooskins roam,
below Mount Himalachia,
Annie Halfpint makes her home.

Her voice booms soft as thunder.
Her hair grows thick as ink.
Her skin feels smooth as gravel.
Her mukluks hold their stink.

Some folks think she's a giant.
She stands just four foot three.
Her mama was an angel,
her pa, a redwood tree.

Way up in Michisota,
Annie's famous far and wide,
because she roped an avalanche
and took it for a ride.

It started on a noonday
in the frigid month of Mace,
when the folks in Yoohoo Valley
held their yearly snowshoe race.

They polished up their parkas.
They saddled up their smiles.
They scaled Mount Himalachia
in the latest snowshoe styles.

As Annie led the plodding pack,
her voice rose sweet as rain.
It rumbled up the mountain
like a locomotive train.

Yodel-ay-hee-hoo

OOOOOOO!

It shook the woolly mooskins.
It shook the piney trees.
It shook ol' Himalachia
and brought it to its knees.

The frosty peaks all grumbled.
The icy-cicles cried.
The snow slipped off the mountain
and slalomed down the side.

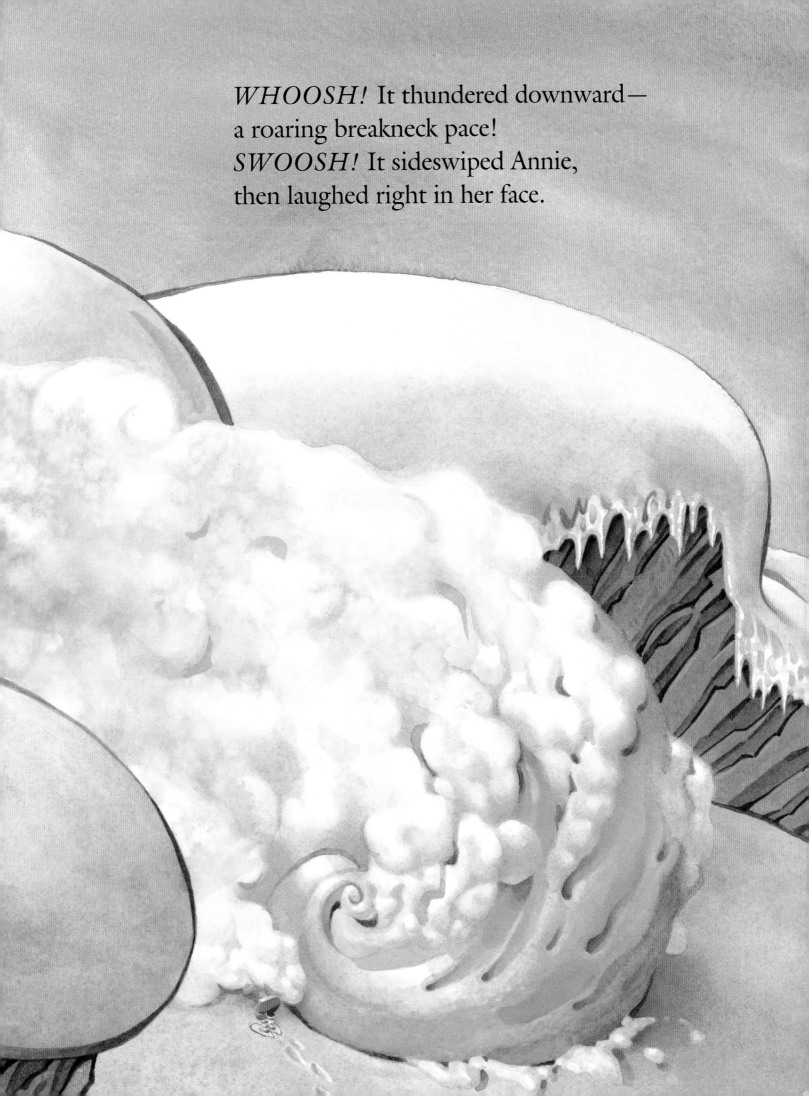

WHOOSH! It thundered downward—
a roaring breakneck pace!
SWOOSH! It sideswiped Annie,
then laughed right in her face.

It circled round the Yoohoos
with taunts and jeering groans,
played hide-and-seek and tweaked their cheeks,
and showered snowball stones.

Annie Halfpint hollered,
"Now halt! You mean ol' cuss!
Back to the top!
                    Hey! I said STOP!
You makin' fun of us?"

Annie tackled from the left.
She felt that slider shift.
It rolled her like a snowy-ball
and dumped her in a drift.

OOOF!

That avalanche was angry—
an awesome icy beast!
That wicked wonder wouldn't stop—
its power had increased!

As Yoohoos scurried downward,
their snowshoes lost their grip.
SNAP! That brute, in close pursuit,
cracked at them like a whip!

Annie took a running leap
and pounced upon its back.

That monstrous mammoth held its own
and countered her attack.

It bucked her like a bronco!
It mauled her like a bear!

It flipped her like a spatula—
she flapjacked through the air!

UMPH!

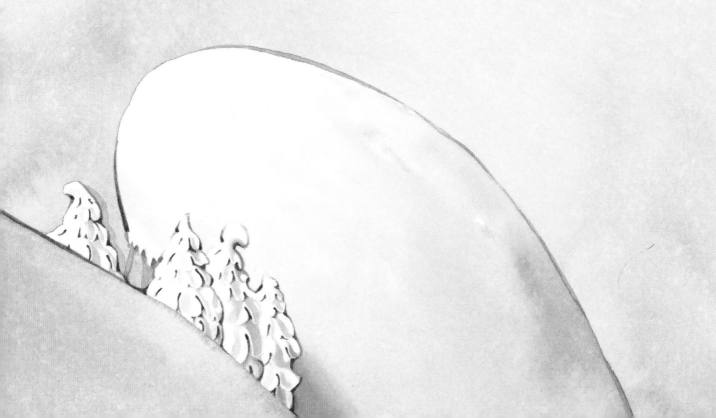

It shot right toward the Yoohoos,
tobogganed down the slope.
It somersaulted through the trees…

…then Annie found a rope.

Annie grabbed that lasso.
(The Yoohoos froze in fright.)
She twirled it like a hoolie-hoop
and tossed with all her might.

Yeeee-ha!

She caught that slick slide-winder.
She tied that shoosher down.
She hitched it like a doggy-sled
and rode it into town.

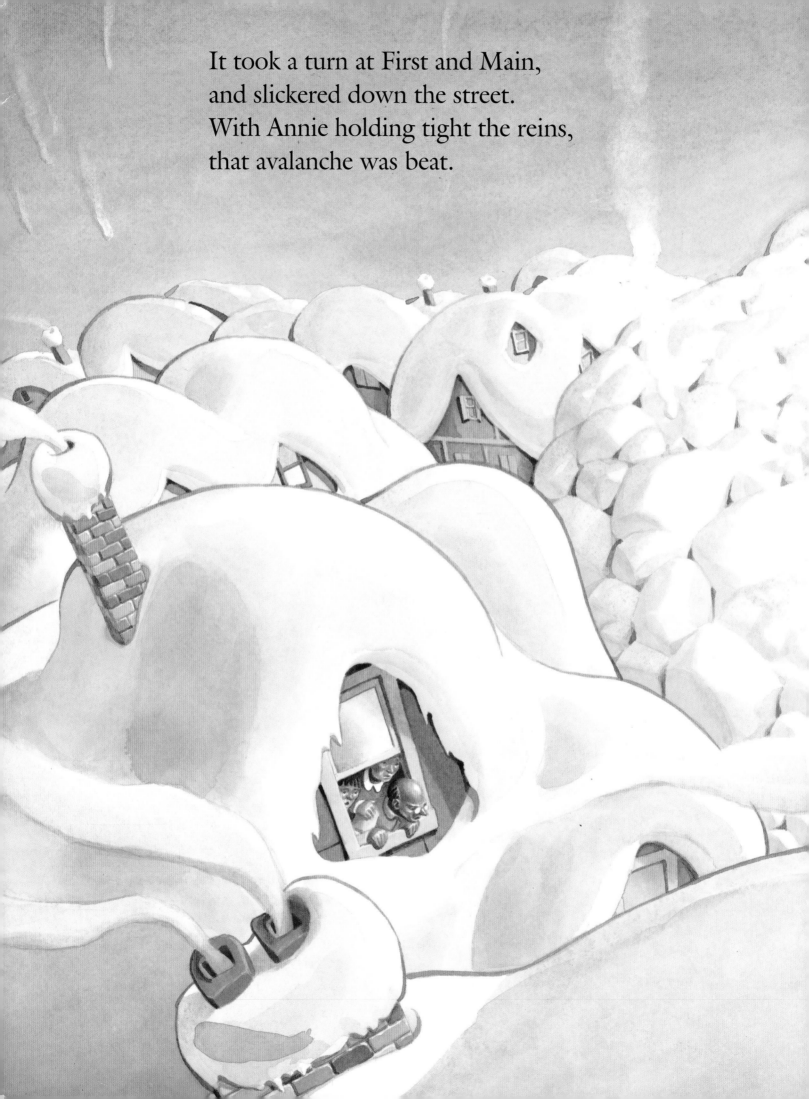

It took a turn at First and Main,
and slickered down the street.
With Annie holding tight the reins,
that avalanche was beat.

It idled on the edge of town
and caused the earth to quake.
It settled in the mossy grove
and formed Twin Antler Lake.

The folks in Yoohoo Valley
all whooped and gave a shout.
"Hoorah for Annie Halfpint!
She rode that mountain out!"

Now Annie's no small legend.
Folks know her far and near.
They named her for that avalanche…